THE GENERAL

Canadian Cataloguing in Publication Data

Etherington, Frank.
  The general

(Annick reading about kids series)
ISBN 0-920236-54-5 (bound). — ISBN 0-920236-55-3 (pbk.)

I. Kurisu, Jane, 1926–   II. Title.   III. Series.

PS8559.T53G46   jC813'.54   C83-098441-0
PZ7.E83Ge

Annick Press gratefully acknowledges the
support of the Canada Council and The
Ontario Arts Council

photo courtesy of Kitchener-Waterloo Record.

Printed and bound in Canada
by Friesen Printers

THE
GENERAL

Frank Etherington
Art · Jane Kurisu

Annick Press Ltd., Toronto, Canada M2N 4Y2

For Jainin and the General.

The Bridgeport General had torn all the buttons off his long coat. He didn't like buttons and he hated zippers. Instead of buttons and zippers, he used large safety pins to close his coat.

When Jainin first met the General, she was six years old and much too shy to speak to him. At home, when she talked to her older brother, Jacob, and her parents, she called him Mr. General.

He got his nickname because of the army-style coat and metal helmet he wore. The helmet was shaped like a flying saucer and had once belonged to a Canadian soldier.

Under his coat, the General wore a leather vest. He didn't have any shirts and, no matter how hot or cold it got in summer or winter, he always had on the same clothes. The only change he ever made was when he left his metal helmet at home and wore a peaked cap that had flaps to keep his ears warm.

He had a battered, home-made stop sign and, for many years, had helped kids cross Lancaster Street on their way to Bridgeport school. Jainin's dad said the General never got paid for his work but did it because he liked kids and wanted something to do with his time.

Jainin was scared of the General when her family first moved to Bridgeport. She thought he looked very strange. Although she never said anything about his clothes, other kids often did.

Some of them shouted cruel names at him and said he looked like a ragbag. The kids would run away when he shook his stop sign at them. If ever anyone asked about his clothes and stayed around long enough to listen, his answer was always the same:

"Look, I wear them because I want to wear them," he said. "Those who think my clothes are stupid wear what they want to wear. Everyone to his own liking. These clothes keep me cool in the summer and warm in the winter."

The General also wore a pair of mitts and large rubber boots.

It was a misty, wet September day when Jainin left home with Jacob to start her first day at school. They walked together down Bridge Street to the crossing. There was a gas station, a butcher's store, a place called the Grand Hotel and a bank with a broken clock at the intersection.

Jainin was sticking her tongue out trying to catch rain dripping off her rain hat when the General met them at the intersection. He noticed Jainin's rubber boots.

"Look at that," he said as the cars and trucks splashed by and rain dribbled down his soldier's helmet. "You got baby General boots."

Under her rain hat, Jainin looked down where her boots poked out the bottom of her long raincoat. She was too shy to answer the General who was measuring one of his boots beside her feet.

"How come your boots are so big?" he asked. "They look too big for your body. You got big feet like me?"

Jainin leaned close to Jacob and didn't say a word.

"She's shy," said Jacob who was eight and a half years old. "Those used to be my boots and she's growing into them. It's her first day at a new school and she's scared. I ain't scared."

"Whatsername," said the General bending down to peek under Jainin's hat.

"Her name's Jainin. It's spelled J.A.I.N.I.N," said Jacob. "She's six and she'll be seven tomorrow 'cos it's her birthday."

"Well Jainin," said the General, careful to say the name correctly, "because you got big feet and General boots and, because it's your birthday tomorrow, I got something special for you."

Jainin looked up as he pushed a glove inside one of his coat pockets.

"Here," he said, "that's for a kid on her first day at new school."

Jainin took the gift but, before she had time to look, the General walked into the middle of the road. With both hands held in the air he stopped two cars and a dump trunk. Jainin, Jacob and some other kids crossed the road and walked up the hill toward their school.

"See you guys at lunchtime," shouted the General. "Don't go rusty in the rain."

When she got to the school playground, Jainin looked down to see what the General had given her.

"Let me see," said Jacob. "It's just a bunch of old beer-bottle caps tied up with wire."

"It's a very pretty bracelet," said Jainin slipping the blue and red bottle caps over her hand.

At school her teacher, Mrs. Schmidt, made name tags for Jainin and two other new kids. She was trying to spell Jainin's name right when she noticed the bracelet.

"Mr. General at the crossing gave it to me," Jainin said.

"The Bridgeport General always has something special for someone on their first day at school," said Mrs. Schmidt. "He's been doing it for as long as I can remember, and I've been here for ten years. It's a lovely bracelet," she said handing Jainin a name tag spelled JANINE.

Other than the name tag, Jainin enjoyed the first day at her new school. She thought the best part of the day was the General's bracelet.

He was there at lunchtime when she ran home. With his head cocked to one side, the General grinned when he saw she was wearing his present.

"Made that myself," he said proudly. "Got the bottlecaps from the hotel. I can make animals out of those caps . . . I'll show you some time."

Jainin wanted to thank him but she was too shy. Instead, she let the General take her hand in his large mitt and walk her across the street.

That evening, when her parents asked about Jainin's first day at school, all they heard about was Mr. General, rubber boots and bottlecap bracelets.

"I guess you found a new friend on your first day," laughed her dad. "You should take Mr. General a chunk of your mom's pie in the morning. I think your friend lives by himself, so I'm sure he'll appreciate it."

The next day, Jainin was carrying a large piece of pie in a plastic bag when she walked to the crossing with Jacob.

"Here comes Jainin, the kid with the General boots," said the General.

"She's got something for you," said Jacob, giving Jainin a nudge in the ear with his elbow. Jainin handed the pie to the General without saying a word.

"What is it?" he asked, crouching down and pushing his hairy face close to Jainin's nose.

"It's a piece of our mom's apple pie," said Jacob.

"Is apple pie your favourite, Jainin?" the General asked.

"No, her favourite is cherry pie," said Jacob.

The General stood up and stared down at Jainin and Jacob. He scratched his beard, tipped his head to one side and looked puzzled.

"How come every time I talk to this little girl, this big guy answers my questions?" said the General.

"You kids be sure and thank your mom. I'll eat the pie for breakfast."

. . .

It was almost a month before Jainin was brave enough to smile at the General and wave when she saw him in the village.

In that time, she found out that he lived alone in a house on Lancaster Street where the paint was peeling, the porch was crooked and most of the windows were smashed or boarded up. The front yard of the house was overgrown with weeds and the backyard was full of rusty junk.

The General used to work at a nearby factory but lost his job when he injured one of his hands. Now, he lived on money he got when he returned pop bottles to Mrs. Grant's corner store. He found the bottles beside the highway and the nearby railway tracks. Once a month, he pushed a shopping cart full of beer bottles to the beer store.

No one ever went inside the General's house where, each night, he sat alone listening to his radio. He told people that he liked listening to the news and weather reports.

Some kids said the General had a barrel full of nickels and dimes inside his house but Jainin's dad said that wasn't true.

As she got to know the General, Jainin began to learn how important it was for him to be a school crossing guard and have a job to do in the village.

Even in the worst snow and freezing rain, she never saw the General miss a day at the intersection.

Jainin also learned that money didn't seem important to the General. Instead of paying for his work as a crossing guard, people in the village took care of him in other ways.

They made him feel good by naming the village park General's Green and changing the name of the street next to his house to General Drive. They also gave him a free doughnut and coffee at the village restaurant every morning.

Jainin was told that a village club, the Bridgeport Clansmen, bought the General oil to keep a small heater burning in his bedroom during the winter.

She stood and watched one day when the Bridgeport police chief used his cruiser to cart away a huge pile of newspapers and junk from the General's backyard because people were worried there might be a fire.

Bridgeport people also gave the General things in return for odd jobs he did. Mrs. Crump, who lived near the intersection, took him a hot meal every Wednesday and Sunday. Jainin often saw her hurrying up the street with the General's meal on a tray.

Even the people who owned the Grand Hotel helped take care of the General. They gave him a bottle of beer and a pickled egg every lunchtime after the kids came home from school.

It didn't seem to trouble the General much when Jainin was too shy to speak. He had sometimes seen her watching when he walked up the railway tracks near her home collecting bottles and he knew that they were friends.

It was different for Jainin to meet older people like the General. She had grandparents but, because they lived a long way away, she saw them only once a year.

Before moving to Bridgeport, Jainin's family had lived in a new subdivision on the outskirts of the nearby city of Kitchener. All of the people that lived in the subdivision were much younger than the General.

It was only when her family moved to the little village by the Grand River that Jainin started to meet older people. She enjoyed being with them because they made her laugh and often did things that kids liked to do.

Jainin also liked them because they were never too busy to listen and seemed to share a problem that most kids had with their parents. The problem was that, every time kids or old people were around, parents became impatient and didn't want to pay attention.

"They're always busy, busy trying to make lots of money and rushing around all over the place," the General told Jainin one day at the crossing. "They never got the time to stop and talk."

One evening, before the General came down the railway track, Jainin found a pop bottle in her garage. She put it on a grass embankment where he was sure to find it. They waved to each other when he picked up the bottle.

A few days later, after the General took Jainin across Lancaster, he told her that she was the last kid home from school that lunchtime.

"So that means it's time for my bottle of beer," he said, turning toward the hotel.

"My tooth fell out in my bed last night," Jainin said.

"Jeepers," said the General, "Jainin can talk. Well, waddya know. Show me the big hole where that tooth came out."

While Jainin stretched her mouth open with both hands, the General got down on one knee to have a good look.

"Pretty soon they're all going to fall out," said Jainin. "My mom says kids' teeth always fall out and then they get new ones."

"Yeah," said the General, "and then, if you don't look after them, those teeth fall out and you don't get new ones. Take a look here at mine."

Jainin moved closer as the General tipped back his head, opened his mouth and showed her his missing teeth.

"That's because I used to open beer bottles with them," he said. "Teeth fall out if you don't look after them. You better make sure you look after yours... and don't go opening beer bottles with them."

The General got up and went into the hotel.

During her first two years at school, Jainin told the General about every tooth that dropped out. He always looked into her mouth to check the hole and, every time she took him a piece of pie or cake, he teased her. He said she was trying to make his few remaining teeth go rotten.

They became the best of friends and Jainin painted dozens of pictures in her art class that showed the General helping kids across the street. He never got tired of the pictures and told her that he nailed them on his kitchen and washroom walls.

The General often sat with Jainin in the parking lot of the Grand Hotel twisting pieces of wire coat hangers into animal shapes. He had a large shoe box full of sparkling bottle caps that he had collected from the hotel. He used a stone and a large nail to make the holes through the centre of the caps and showed Jainin how to thread the caps on the wire.

Jainin had a collection of bottle-cap animals in her bedroom. Her favourite was a giraffe which had a blue and yellow striped neck, a red body and green legs.

During winter months, when she wasn't too busy with homework, Jainin took her small snow shovel and helped the General clear snow from driveways and sidewalks. When people offered the General money for his work, he always gave the same reply.

"Don't bother. Send me a postcard when you go on holidays. I don't need money. Just send me a letter or card."

He told Jainin he had never been on vacation but liked to get letters in the mail. His favourite postcards had pictures of people smiling on sunny beaches and kids splashing in the ocean.

When the cards arrived, they were addressed to The General, Bridgeport, Ontario. Because the village mailman knew the General so well, his mail always arrived safely at his home.

Jainin also helped the General search for bottles around the village. Some days they would walk along the river bank picking up garbage and collecting bottles.

The General knew every inch of the river where it flowed through the village. When they walked by the water he would sometimes tell Jainin to be very quiet and show her a muskrat's home or a spot among the reeds where a family of ducks was nesting. He also showed her the traps that someone set to catch the muskrat and laughed every time he used a stick to spring the traps.

"There, that miserable old trapper won't catch anything in that one," he would say as the trap snapped shut.

The General often talked about what the river looked like when he was Jainin's age.

"We would all come down here, make a raft and go fishing or diving or swimming. The water was clean enough to drink. Now look at it. Who would swim in there, let along drink it?"

Jainin and the General were always cleaning junk out of the river. One day they used a branch to pull two tires and part of a mattress out of the water.

At school, Jainin told her environment class about the General's clean-up work and suggested that the kids help tidy up the river bank. Her teacher agreed and, once a week that summer, Jainin's class went out and searched for garbage beside the river.

The General was pleased to see the river looking cleaner but grumbled that the kids did such a good job, there were only a few bottles left for him to find.

Once, when Jainin and the General were walking near the railway tracks, they found a wallet full of money. They took it to the village police chief who returned the wallet and money to a man who worked on the railway.

A few days later the General went to Jainin's house while she was at school. He told her mom that the man who owned the wallet had sent a $10 reward.

"Jainin helped find it so I brought her $5," he said.

When Jainin got home she said she would spend the money on a birthday present for the General.

"I don't think he gets many presents. The problem is, I don't know when his birthday is," she said.

"Ask him," said her dad. So she did.

"When's yours?" asked the General.

"September the second," answered Jainin.

"Can't remember when I was born," he said. "I just know it was a long, long time ago."

Jainin told him that if he couldn't remember he could share her birthday.

When September 2nd arrived he gave her a silver pocketwatch that didn't work, wrapped in a piece of soft velvet. Jainin went to the drug store and bought him a package of large safety pins after she noticed that the ones on his coat were getting rusty.

Because the General was so pleased with his birthday gift, Jainin told her family she was going to get him a special Christmas present. During the next few months she spent a lot of time thinking about what she could give to the General.

"I know he doesn't like new clothes so I can't get that kind of stuff," she told her mom, "and he doesn't shave very much so I can't get him that stinky stuff dad puts on his face."

Jainin's mom suggested that the General might like a card or picture that Jainin could paint at school. Jainin said he already had too many of her pictures.

One afternoon, when Jainin was home from school on a teacher-training day, her mom took her Christmas shopping in the city. When the bus passed a school crossing guard in Kitchener, Jainin suddenly had an idea.

"That's what I could get him. He doesn't have a very good stop sign. I could make him one."

"You could do it in the garage this weekend," her mom said. "I'm sure your dad has stuff you could use to make a sign."

Jainin's dad thought the stop sign was a great idea for a present. Together they searched through the garage that night and found some red paint, a handle

from an old snow shovel and a metal circle her dad had brought home from the hardware store where he worked.

On Friday evening, Jainin spread out some newspapers in the garage and found herself a paint brush. Before she went to bed, she painted the metal circle

Later, while her dad helped to scrub paint off her fingers, Jainin explained how she would borrow her mom's stencils to write letters on the sign. Jacob glanced up from a comic book he was reading and said she could use a can of white paint he had bought to decorate his bike.

The next day, when the red paint was dry, Jainin arranged the stencils on the metal circle and wrote STOP with the white paint. She used a saw to cut a slot in the top of the snow-shovel handle and a nail to attach the handle to the red circle.

After lunch, she wrapped up the sign and made a Christmas card to tell the General that the sign was a present from her family.

The General was chipping ice from the sidewalk outside Mrs. Crump's house when Jacob and Jainin took him the gift on Christmas Eve morning.

"This is for you, for Christmas," Jainin said.

The General stopped his work and looked at the huge parcel.

"You're kidding," he said, "What's in there? A new snow shovel?"

"You're not supposed to see it until Christmas but, because we won't see you, we want you to open it now," said Jainin.

"Well, let's get in here out of the wind," he said, leading Jainin and Jacob into the shelter of Mrs. Crump's porch. He put down his shovel and looked at the package.

The General had difficulty undoing the string around the parcel because he didn't take off his leather mitts. Jainin and Jacob helped him untie the knots.

"I'll be..." said the General, when he saw the sign, "ain't you kids nice, ain't you nice."

He looked like he wanted to hug them but didn't know how. Instead, he did a very strange thing.

"You kids going home now?" he asked.

"Yes," said Jainin, "we have other presents to wrap."

"That means you have to go across the street, right? So that'll give me a chance to try my new sign," he said.

"But there's no school," said Jainin.

"And no cars coming," added Jacob.

"Don't matter," said the General. "We'll just wait for some cars."

He took Jainin and Jacob down to the intersection and waited in the snow until a bus came down the street.

The General walked out waving his new sign while the bus driver stopped, honked his horn and opened his passenger doors. People on the bus clapped and cheered when they saw the new stop sign.

"Finally got yourself a decent sign?" laughed the bus driver.

"Yep, just got it from these kids for Christmas," said the General. Then he marched Jainin and Jacob across to the opposite side of the street.

All that day, he used the new sign to stop traffic every time Christmas shoppers wanted to cross the street. Jainin's dad said the General was still stopping cars when he drove home from work.

From that day on, the General carried the sign that Jainin made for him. When he wasn't using the sign, he kept it propped in a corner of the porch at his house.

. . .

One morning Jainin was on her way to school with Jacob when she noticed that the General wasn't at the crossing. She was worried because she knew he never missed a day at the intersection. Glancing up Lancaster toward the General's house, Jainin couldn't see her friend.

"He wouldn't miss a day and he never sleeps in," she said to Jacob. "Maybe he's sick and no one knows."

Jacob said they had some time before school began, so they went to see what had happened to the General. As they walked toward the house, Jainin could smell smoke.

She looked up at a bedroom window. It had been covered with a sheet of plywood ever since one of the kids, who teased the General, threw a stone and smashed the glass.

"There's smoke coming out of his bedroom window," Jainin shouted. She began to run toward the house. Before she reached the General's front door, the plywood was suddenly smashed out of the window and fell with a crash onto the porch.

"Get help, I can't breathe," gasped the General as he leaned out of his window surrounded by black smoke.

"We're coming," screamed Jainin.

"I'll try to get inside. You get someone to phone the fire department," shouted Jacob.

Jainin could see traffic coming down Lancaster. When she waved her arms and tried to stop a car, the driver didn't see her. She rushed back to the porch and grabbed the STOP sign.

Jacob was trying to get the front door open as she picked up the sign and dashed back to the street.

"The door won't open, I'm going around back," Jacob shouted.

Jainin ran up the street and waved the sign until a truck stopped.

"The General's house is on fire," she called out, "phone the fire department, get an ambulance."

"Don't worry kid, I'll use my CB radio. You get back on the sidewalk," the truck driver shouted.

Jainin could hear the man radioing for help as she dashed to the house. When she went around to the back, Jacob was trying to get a window open.

Finally it opened with a bang. Jacob was climbing into the house when a fireman ran into the backyard.

"You kids get out of there! We'll get him out. Get around to the front and stay there," the fireman shouted as he pulled on an oxygen mask and climbed through the window.

When Jainin and Jacob went to the front of the house, the firemen already had a ladder up to the General's bedroom window and an ambulance with a flashing light had just arrived. One fireman was at the top of the ladder, peering into the smoke.

"It's OK, not serious, just a pile of clothes making lots of smoke," he called as he disappeared into the General's bedroom. He was throwing smouldering clothes out of the window when the fireman who had climbed in the back window brought the General out of the house.

"His feet are badly burned," the fireman said to an ambulance attendant. "Get a stretcher over here."

Three men helped lift the General on the stretcher and carried him toward the ambulance. Jainin was shivering and began to cry as she watched the stretcher go by.

The General opened his eyes and called Jainin and Jacob over just before the men lifted him into the ambulance.

"Don't worry, I'll be back soon. None of that stuff," he said as he wiped away a tear from Jainin's cheek. "Get off to school and do my crossing-guard work until I get back."

As the ambulance pulled away, Jacob put an arm around Jainin's shoulder.

"Come on, let's go to school," she said.

Later that day Jainin's teacher, Mr. Chambers, told the class what had happened. He said the school was proud of the way Jainin and Jacob had helped the General.

"I checked with the hospital and he's going to be OK. He put his socks out to dry on the oil heater in his bedroom and the thing caught fire," he said. "He burned his feet trying to stomp out the flames and the doctor says he'll be in the hospital for a couple of weeks."

Jainin asked her teacher if the kids could make some cards for the General and send them to the hospital. Mr. Chambers said that because Jainin was a special friend of the General, she could go with him to the hospital to deliver the cards.

When they arrived at the General's hospital room, he looked very different without his helmet, coat and rubber boots.

Usually his hair stuck out from under his helmet because he didn't like combs and hairbrushes. He always had the prickles of a grey beard covering his chin and cheeks but, in the hospital, his face was shaved and looked pink.

The General was sitting up in bed complaining about having to wash so much. "Wash that much and you get sick," he told a nurse. "You get nothing but colds. I washed yesterday and that's plenty for a while."

The nurse smiled and told him not to be such a grouch. She was puffing up his pillows when Jainin and Mr. Chambers walked into the room. The General was pleased to see them and said he would spend the rest of the day reading the cards.

Mr. Chambers told the General to stay in bed and take care of himself until his feet healed.

"I could stay in bed at home. I'd like to get out of here. What's happening with the kids? Who's getting them across the street?" asked the General.

"Jacob and I are taking turns," said Jainin. "We borrowed your sign. We all want you back, but you have to get your feet better."

When visiting time was over, Jainin and Mr. Chambers met a doctor as they were leaving the room.

"Friends of the grumpy, grouchy, General?" the doctor asked.

Jainin and Mr. Chambers laughed and asked when the General would be back on his feet.

"Shouldn't be long," the doctor replied. "He's a tough guy and he's hard to keep in bed. He's got minor burns and we could probably send him home but we're afraid he won't take care of himself."

. . .

When the General came back to the village things returned to normal at the intersection. Jainin was often busy now with homework and didn't see much of her friend until the summer arrived.

One Saturday she was sitting with him near the Grand Hotel when they saw a truck from the City of Kitchener pull up beside a road sign. The sign said "Bridgeport, Population 502." The men climbed out of the truck and began to dig the sign posts out of the ground.

Jainin and the General walked over to the men and asked what they were doing.

"There's no such place as Bridgeport any more," one man said. "You guys live in Kitchener now, so we're taking the Bridgeport sign away.

"But this is Bridgeport," said Jainin. "You must have made a mistake."

"Not any more it ain't," said the man throwing the sign in the back of the truck. "Now, it's part of Kitchener."

Then they climbed in the truck and drove away.

"They think that because they take a sign down and make some rules people will think there ain't no

Bridgeport," the General said. "I heard on the radio news that Bridgeport is being joined to Kitchener, but taking away signs won't make people stop thinking they live in Bridgeport. It's the people that makes the place and taking down signs don't make no difference. This will always be Bridgeport. Some things don't change."

At school the next day Jainin asked her teacher about Bridgeport becoming part of Kitchener. He said there were a few small villages around Kitchener that were being joined to the city. Once they were joined, a larger government would be made for the whole area.

He said Jainin had nothing to worry about.

"Our school will still be called Bridgeport School. We won't have our own village council or police chief but you'll hardly see any difference. Most things won't change," he said.

But Jainin soon found out that the General and her teacher were wrong. Things did change and the biggest change was that Kitchener didn't have a place for the Bridgeport General.

It was a hot summer day, when Jainin found the General in the empty hotel parking lot. He was sitting on a wooden box near the garbage containers.

Walking across the dusty gravel, she could see her friend grinding the handle of his school crossing-guard sign into the dirt. He was shaking his head and muttering.

As she came closer, swinging an empty beer bottle in each hand, she could see a crumpled piece of paper in one of his mitts. He seemed upset about something and, when he turned toward her, his eyes looked red above his beard.

Jainin was now 11 years old and, although she'd been the General's friend for years, she had never seen him so angry and upset. She put the bottles down beside his rubber boots.

"I found two bottles for you up by the river bridge."

He shifted so she could sit beside him and Jainin looked down at the crumpled letter in his hand. The letter was typed and addressed to the General but the person who sent it had used her friend's real name, Frank Groff. The letter came from the man in charge of school-crossing guards at the city of Kitchener.

"Dear Mr. Groff," the letter said, "our department is in charge of school crossing guards in Kitchener and is responsible for the safety of school children in the area.

As you know, Bridgeport recently became part of Kitchener. This gave our department the added responsibility for school children in your village. We appreciate your voluntary work for the past 18 years, but our crossing-guard inspector has brought certain concerns to our attention.

He reports that, when he visited your crossing, you refused to wear the official uniform supplied to all guards. You also refused to use a regulation Stop sign instead of your home-made sign.

Our inspector says that you will not wear a wrist watch and occasionally arrive late at the intersection. One lunch time, you were seen to leave the crossing early, before all of the children were safely across the road.

You told our inspector 'All the kids are gone now, it's time for a drink.' Our inspector says that you then went into the Grand Hotel for a bottle of beer . . ."

Jainin looked up and saw the General watching her closely.

"My eyes ain't so good. You understand that stuff? They say I ain't safe. I been helping kids cross the streets for all those years and no one ever got hurt, so what do they mean by this?"

Jainin glanced down to the part of the letter the General was stabbing with his mitt. It said he took children into the road without giving enough warning to people driving cars and trucks.

"Our inspector reports that your dress and cleanliness are also not acceptable," the letter said.

"For these reasons, you are no longer needed as a crossing guard after the summer break."

Sitting beside her friend in the parking lot, Jainin was so angry about the letter she crumpled it into a ball and threw it over the General's head into a garbage container.

"That's rotten, they can't do that. We need you for our crossing guard," she said.

"You're a darling," muttered the General, "but those guys got rules and regulations and uniforms and numbers and all that crazy stuff. I ain't got time for that nonsense."

"But that's your job and you like it so much," said Jainin. "You're our friend and what they're doing isn't right. You're the best crossing guard in the whole world."

"Look, I been wearing this stuff all my life," said the General. "I don't tell anyone else they got to be the same as me. I ain't wearing no uniform and don't need no watch. I ain't jumping when they say jump and I don't need their money...I'll have to find something else to do, but I don't know about much else."

Jainin wanted time to think and didn't want her friend to see her cry. She told the General she would see him later and walked home. When she got to her house, she went to her bedroom and took out the bottle-cap giraffe and broken watch the General had given her. She was still in her room when her dad came home from work.

Jainin heard his car arrive but didn't feel like going to meet him. After he talked to her mom, he came upstairs to Jainin's room.

"Jainin in her junk room," he teased, "what's the long face for?"

When she didn't look up, he sat beside her on the bed and asked about her day.

"They're going to take the General's job away," she said. "The people in Kitchener are taking away his cross-guard job just because he won't wear a stupid uniform and carry their ugly sign."

"Hold on, hold on," said her dad. "Now, tell me slowly what's been happening."

Jainin explained everything. When she finished, her dad was very quiet and very angry. "He's been at that crossing for a long while and no kids have been hurt. They come in here, take over the village and tell us the guy's no good because he happens to be old and dresses differently. It's just not fair," he said.

"I'm not going to sit around and let them do that to my friend," said Jainin. "None of the kids will. We'll get a petition, a long list of people who want the General to stay, and they'll have to listen. They can't get rid of the General."

Her dad put an arm around her shoulders. "Good for you, Jainin. People like the General are precious and are worth fighting for."

That night Jainin and Jacob wrote the petition: "To Kitchener Council and the person in charge of school-crossing guards. We don't want the Bridgeport General fired from his job as school-crossing guard. We want Kitchener to give the General back his job because he has worked as a school-crossing guard for 18 years and not one kid has ever been hurt in an accident."

Jainin's friend, Lisa, used her mom's copying machine to make six petitions. Jainin and her friends left copies at the butcher's shop, the hotel, the post office and the village council office. Jainin's dad took one to work and the kids took another petition to school for teachers to sign.

That night, Jainin and her friends met in her garage to think of other things they could do to help the General to keep his job. Lisa said someone should call the newspaper and the television station to tell them what was happening.

"How about making some big signs?" suggested Jacob. "We could march up and down at the intersection."

By the time the meeting ended, everything was arranged. Jainin was in charge of collecting petitions, Lisa said she would phone the newspaper and TV and the other kids said they would help Jacob to make signs.

When Jainin went to collect the petitions and added up the names, she found there were almost 300 people who wanted the General to keep his job.

That weekend the kids borrowed hammers, nails and pieces of wood. They met at the school playground to make the signs.

The signs said, "Bring back the General," and, "We want the General."

On Monday morning Jainin and her friends got up early and carried the signs to the intersection. The General stood and grinned while the kids marched up and down. Lisa had called the newspaper and photographers were there to take pictures.

The Spectator

The General told to leave

KITCHENER. —

Frank Groff 'The General' seen here with loyal friends. Kitchener City Council wants to replace Mr. Groff.

Jainin's sign said, "If you love the General, honk your horn." All the car and truck drivers, who had seen the General at the intersection for years, honked so much the kids could hardly hear themselves talk.

Reporters asked the General about his job and photographers took pictures of him carrying his stop sign surrounded by kids.

That night, a picture and story about the General were on the front page of the newspaper. A film that showed the children carrying their signs was also on the TV news.

The mayor of Kitchener was interviewed on the radio. She said she would like to help the General but she was worried that children would get hurt if he continued to work as crossing guard in Bridgeport. She said it was up to council members to decide what would happen to the General.

Council called a special meeting to talk about whether the General could keep his job. When Jainin and Jacob heard about the meeting, they talked to Mr. Brubacher who ran the village garage and owned a bus that took people on trips. Mr. Brubacher said he would take a busload of people to the meeting in Kitchener.

"I want to be there myself to tell them they have no right to do this to our General," he said.

Erwin Cronmiller, the Bridgeport mayor, Mrs. Grant from the village corner store, Mrs. Crump and Jainin's school principal, Mr. Stephenson, were among the adults who said they wanted to go to the meeting. Jainin's mom and dad said they wouldn't miss it for anything.

On the bus trip to Kitchener city hall, everyone sang songs. Just before they arrived, Mr. Cronmiller walked back to Jainin's seat.

"We've been given time for three people to speak," he said. "I'll be first and your dad will say a few words. Then you speak for the kids and give them your petition, Jainin," he said.

The council meeting was on the second floor in a large room where the councillors sat at a table shaped like a horseshoe. The mayor's chair was at the centre of the horseshoe and looked like a king's throne.

They had to bring in more chairs because so many people came from Bridgeport.

When Mr. Cronmiller was asked to speak, he said Bridgeport wouldn't be Bridgeport without the General. He said Kitchener council should be glad that people like the General would do such a good job and not expect to be paid. He also said that Kitchener council should not fire the General because his clothes were different.

When he finished talking, Mrs. Crump clapped her hands and stomped her feet.

Jainin's dad told council that the General cared about the safety of all children. He said he had checked with the village police chief and found that there had never been a child hurt at the crossing. When her dad sat down, Jainin's throat was very dry and her stomach was making groaning noises. She was very nervous.

"Now we will hear from one of the children who have been so busy making us look like bad guys and trying to help the General," the Kitchener mayor said with a smile.

Jainin stood up and walked to the front of the meeting. She handed the petition to the nearest councillor and cleared her throat.

"The General is our friend and loves his job," she said. "It's the only thing he knows how to do. He says he's got to have something to do. We'd like to keep him as our crossing guard."

After Jainin sat down, the councillors said they were grateful for the General's work and thought it was good that he had so many friends. But then they said they had to replace him with another guard because they had to be certain that the kids were safe at the crossing.

When they voted, the councillors decided that the General would not keep his job.

Some of the people from Bridgeport began to boo and shout that council had no right to treat the General so badly. When that happened, the mayor of Kitchener banged a wooden hammer on her desk and asked everyone to leave the room.

Back on Mr. Brubacher's bus, the people from Bridgeport were so upset they didn't talk very much. Lisa sat beside a window staring out into the darkness and Jainin could see that her friend was close to tears.

She reached over and took Lisa's hand as Mr. Stephenson walked back to their seat. He said they should not feel badly about what had happened.

"You did everything you could and you should feel good about that. We'll just have to find the General something else to keep him busy," he said. "Don't worry, we'll find something."

Jainin and Lisa couldn't talk. They knew there wasn't anything else that the General wanted to do.

No one sang on the way home.

. . .

The next day was Saturday and Jainin was on her way to the corner store when she met the General. When he saw how sad she looked, he smiled and put a hand on her shoulder.

"I heard what all you people did in Kitchener and it made me feel like a real somebody," he said.

"Didn't do much good, though," said Jainin staring at her feet.

"Don't you believe it. You kids are in for a big surprise. Wait until Monday, you'll see. They're not getting rid of me that easy," he said. "I been here too long for that."

"But they say they won't let you do your job any more," said Jainin, "and they won't listen to us."

"Just you wait, girl," he said. "They took away the Bridgeport sign but this is still Bridgeport, right?"

Jainin didn't understand but, on Monday morning, she got up early to see what would happen at the crossing.

When Jainin, Jacob and their friends arrived at the intersection, a woman stood in the middle of the road wearing a new crossing-guard uniform and carrying a City of Kitchener stop sign. The General still wore his old clothes and carried his home-made sign.

With a warm smile on her face the woman linked arms with the General when she saw the kids coming. They laughed together like old friends as they used both signs to stop the traffic. When they marched the cheering kids across Lancaster, the woman put her hand on Jainin's shoulder.

"Don't worry, we've got everything all worked out. Years ago the General helped my kids across this street on their way to your school. He's a great guy and he refuses to go away," she said. "You kids will be extra safe from now on because you'll have two crossing guards."

Jainin glanced up at the grinning General.

"Told them I wasn't going to quit doing my work," he said. "This lady understands that. She's really nice and, when you all get to know her better, we're going to call her the General's helper."

Pupils baking for The General

FEB 1974

The Bridgeport General will get some cookies this Valentine's Day.

And, sometime this week, he will also get about 60 get-well-soon cards and letters delivered to a room at K-W Hospital where he is recovering from burns to his feet.

The General, Frank Groff, 60, has acted as a self-appointed, unofficial school crossing guard every day for the past 16 years at Lancaster and Bridge Streets, Bridgeport. He is well known for the rubber boots, gloves, cap

and long winter coat he wears in all weather.

On Monday a bedroom heater at his rambling old Lancaster and Oak Streets home caused a small fire. The General tried to stomp it out with his feet, burned himself, and was taken to hospital by police.

"The children all like him and have missed him for the past few days," said Debbie Schweiger, a pupil at Bridgeport public. She said tw...

six- and seven-year-old children decided to prepare cards and letters and also voted to give The General some of the Valentine cookies they plan to bake.

The General, in hospital in satisfactory condition, hopes to be back home in a week.

Meanwhile, Kitchener fire prevention officers, who inspected the house after the fire, say they would request that conditions creating a fire hazard be cleaned up before the General gets home.

The Bridgeport General is captured on canvas

MAY 2 1978

By TRISH WILSON
Record Staff Writer

The Bridgeport General captured the imagination of a lot of people, but Frank Psutka has done something about it.

The young artist had heard stories about the eccentric Frank Groff — who worked as an unofficial school crossing guard at the corner of Lancaster and Bridge streets until his death at 64 this January — but he didn't catch his first glimpse of him until two years ago.

Psutka, now 23, was fascinated.

"As soon as I saw him everything started to go through my mind," he said. "I knew I had something good here. He had so much character."

So important Psutka felt the project was that he didn't intend to embark on it lightly.

First he engineered a meeting on the street with the General to ask his permission to take some color slides he could use to work from.

"I didn't really know what to expect when I first met him,"

he said. "But he seemed pleased about the idea — and, of course, he was inquisitive about me — being in a wheelchair."

Psutka has been confined to a wheelchair since he was five years old, when a sudden and mysterious affliction which confounded his doctors left him paralyzed from the waist down.

A graduate of the vocational art course at Cameron Heights collegiate, Psutka originally planned to go into commercial art when he got "hooked" on fine art.

For the last four years, then, since graduation, he has concentrated on becoming a painter.

He lives at 476 Duke St. W. with his parents, Carl and Sophie Psutka and a younger sister.

His studio is his meticulously neat bedroom, where he polishes the difficult techniques to create paintings in an almost photo-realist style.

The idea of the General portrait was put aside until last October because Frank

didn't feel he was ready to do it.

"I postponed him to get more experience in oils. . . until I thought I could handle him," he explained.

The portrait, painstakingly painted in oils, took five months to complete.

Sixty by 38 inches in dimension, it shows the General wearing a quizzical look — and his year-round uniform of safety-pinned army coat, mittens, rubber boots, dungarees and rakish ragged cap.

It's not the first portrait. Psutka has also done pencil sketches and scrape-a-board and is thinking of making some etchings of the General and then producing a limited edition of prints.

Right now, however, Psutka's first aim is to get the large portrait out into a show-place. So far he's had no luck. Galleries are booked until the fall at the earliest, Psutka said.

Eventually, he'd like to sell the work. One of the first steps toward supporting himself as an artist.

400 sign petition urging rehiring of the General

MAR 12 1974

A 400-signature petition asking for reinstatement of the Bridgeport General as a school-crossing guard has delayed Kitchener's plans to recognize the General for his 16 years of service to the Bridgeport area.

Kitchener council agreed Monday to table the issue until supporters of Frank Groff, 60, of 559 Lancaster St., have studied the staff report, which outlines reasons for his dismissal Feb. 28 from the crossing-guard service.

Two delegations appeared before council on the General's behalf, stating that he had done a good job directing children at Lancaster and Bridge Streets.

Mrs. Henry Hartman of 35 Schweitzer St. and Don M~ Pherson of 41 Lang-C~ people in the Bri~ want the Gen~ job.

Mr. ~
re~

~ said the General's salary is not the important issue, but rather his pride in having a job and a position in the community.

"We ask you to give serious consideration to the human aspects of this situation."

Mr. Groff served as a crossing guard without pay for 15 years. When the city annexed Bridgeport in January, 1973, he was given a $150-monthly wage, the same as other crossing guards.

The traffic department report on his firing said the General constitutes a hazard to himself, the children and traffic because of his poor reaction to traffic flow.

He also reported for duty late, left early, failed to advise the department when he would be absent, refused to wear safety clothing and ~uldn't use a regulation stop the report said.

MacPherson said the village council didn't Groff a uniform or a when he first as-

~sumed responsibility for the intersection because the village did not have any.

The General carries a stop sign, which someone gave him, but has repeatedly refused to wear the regulation safety vest and hat that other Kitchener crossing guards wear.

He is known for the rubber boots, long coat, gloves, cap and dungarees he wears in all weather.

Ald. Al Barron said that at first he was opposed to the firing, but after reading the staff report he agreed the city had no alternative.

"If every parent whose child uses the crossing wishes to absolve the city of any responsibility, I'm all for putting him back on the job," he said.

Ald. Merv Villemaire said council was not concerned about the General's dress, but about the safety of the children.

But Ald. Morley Rosenberg said the city has almost completely ignored the General's safety record. There have been no reports of accidents involving children at the intersection since the General took over.

Ald. George Mitchell thought the issue should be handled by the city administration. "We're making a political football out of one of our personnel . . . holding a person up for a public spectacle. And I think that's wrong."

Mr. Groff's supporters ~reed to return to council in ~ weeks after they have ~ed the staff report.

Bridgeport Lions may help repair General's roof

BY FRANK ETHERINGTON
Record Staff Writer

A local service club may help the Bridgeport General pay for roof repairs at his house.

Executive members of the Bridgeport Lions Club will decide tonight whether to set up a fund to help the General.

The eccentric General had saved for more than a year to fix the leaking roof at his Bridgeport home but thieves broke into his house and stole his money.

"We really feel for the guy," said Brian Schell, Lions club secretary. "We've helped him before and we're definitely considering how we can help him now."

Mr. Schell said the club ~

~come perhaps co-ordinate some kind of fund" to help the General.

Club members will discuss tonight an offer from a Bridgeport roofer to provide free labor at the General's house.

In past years the service club has attempted to take care of the General — renowned as the unofficial and unpaid school crossing guard at Lancaster and Bridge Streets.

The club bought the General a propane furnace for his home and arranged regular checks to eliminate fire hazards at Mr. Groff's home.

The General — known for his year-round dress of rubber boots, dungarees, cap and safety-pinned ex-army coat — lives on a small pension and money he collects by cashing in pop and beer bottles he finds around Bridgeport.

For about 18 years he has provided the voluntary crossing-guard service.

57

It's work as usual for fired General

By FRANK ETHERINGTON
Record Staff Writer

Hobbling along the expressway embankment near Bridgeport, the General stooped in the pouring rain to pick up an empty Coke bottle and vowed he wouldn't abandon his school-crossing guard work.

"I started it. It's the only thing that people appreciate me doing. I've been helping those little devils across the street for a long, long time and I don't intend to give it up," he said.

The General, Frank Groff, 60, of 559 Lancaster St., was commenting his firing by the City of Kitchener from his position as school-crossing guard at Lancaster and Bridge Streets.

"I don't care what they say, I'm still going back there every day. They tell me not to interfere but I don't see why we couldn't take turns to get the kids across. I don't give a damn if they pay me or not. I just want something to do.

gotta do something with my time," he said.

When he isn't a "crossing" the General "hunts" discarded pop and beer bottles in the Bridgeport area. He also shovels snow for several widows and pensioners in the village and picks up glass and garbage from hotel parking lots.)

The General, who lives alone, has been replaced by Betty Ann Bagley of Kitchener. Today the General showed up as usual at his post but was told not to take children across the road.

"It's OK with the woman if I take some kids across, but not with the city. Regardless what you do it's not good enough for some."

The General was fired because of concern for children's safety and because the eccentric would not conform to regulations.

He had been a crossing guard at the intersection for the past 16 years and for 15 of those years worked without pay.

GENERAL'S AIDE—Bridgeport's eccentric General Groff showed up as usual today for school-crossing guard duty at Lancaster and Bridge Streets despite being fired by the City of Kitchener and replaced by Betty Bagley of W........... Photo by Jim Goodwin

MAR 4 1974

58

Park named after General

Seven years after Kitchener fired the Bridgeport General from his job as unofficial crossing guard, city planners voted Monday to name a park after the eccentric.

The General's Green is at Lancaster and Bridge Streets where Frank Groff, dubbed the General, acted as school crossing guard for more than 20 years.

Kitchener plans to spend about $11,000 on the small piece of vacant land.

City parks commissioner Fred Graham told planners the suggested name for the park was appropriate because the General was so well known in the area.

He said using the General's real name would not be appropriate because so few people knew him by that name.

The General was fired from his voluntary work after regional government made the village of Bridgeport part of Kitchener.

He was fired because he refused to wear an official crossing guard's uniform and carry an official stop sign.

Since his death, the General has had a Bridgeport street and a local hotel lounge named after him.

His color portrait hangs outside the office of Kitchener Mayor Morley Rosenberg and his picture is featured on t-shirts sold in a Bridgeport pub.

The t-shirts say University of Bridgeport.

Pupils plan memorial to General

By FRANK ETHERINGTON
Record Staff Writer

School kids in Bridgeport don't plan to forget their General.

The General — Frank Groff, 64 — died Tuesday at K-W Hospital after acting as unofficial, and for many years unpaid, school crossing guard for Bridgeport children during the past 20 years.

The kids, from Bridgeport public and St. Anthony separate schools, missed The General at the busy Lancaster and Bridge Streets intersection Monday and were sad to hear he was sick in hospital.

Funeral services were held for The General in Kitchener today and the flag flew at half mast at Bridgeport public school.

At school, the kids were busy collecting money to buy a memorial plaque which will be named after their eccentric crossing guard.

Bruce McFarlane, school principal, said staff and students wanted some way to remember Groff.

The plaque will be presented every year to the student considered the best safety-patrol officer at road intersections near the school.

McFarlane said a donation would also be sent to the K-W Rotary children's centre as requested by relatives organizing The General's funeral.

"We wanted to remember him — he was a great old guy — and this seemed a good way to do it," said the principal, adding that the plaque will be displayed along with pictures of The General.

The pictures show The General outside his dilapidated home at 559 Lancaster St. W. carrying his home-made STOP sign. He's wearing the cap, safety-pinned coat, gloves, dungarees and rubber boots that became his trademark in winter and summer for motorists driving through Bridgeport.

In previous years, The General said most kids he dealt with were "little devils, but good." What he said about the bad ones could never be printed.

Asked about the few kids who taunted or threw stones at him over the years, The General said: "I don't bother with them — they got nothing better they can do."

The empathy he had with kids were never more apparent than when Kitchener took over Bridgeport and replaced The General as crossing guard.

The city said The General was not doing a good job at the crossing and would not wear an official crossing-guard uniform.

The city was immediately faced with a Bridgeport demonstration where school kids carried picket signs demanding the return of The General. More than 400 residents protested the city's decision.

Through it all Frank Groff went about business as usual.

He had no time for the uniform and dealt with the dismissal in typical fashion — he ignored it and continued to show up at the intersection as usual, duplicating the efforts of the city's new crossing guard.

At the time he said he "didn't give a damn what the city said."

"I'm going back there whether they pay me or not. The kids need me and I gotta have something to do with my time. I'm going back there every day."

That was in 1974. School kids saw him come back every day until Monday.

59

Frank Etherington was born in England. He came
to Canada in 1967, and worked as a journalist in
Toronto, before moving to Kitchener, Ontario,
where he met THE GENERAL.
Frank has won several newspaper awards. His
previous children's books are THE SPAGHETTI
WORD RACE and THOSE WORDS.

Jane Kurisu was born and educated in Toronto, Ontario. A graduate of Sheridan College of Visual Arts, Jane has worked as freelance illustrator and graphic designer in Los Angeles, London and Toronto.
For the past four years Jane and her family have made their home in Ottawa.

Distributed in Canada and the USA by:
Firefly Books Ltd.
3520 Pharmacy Avenue, Unit 1-C
Scarborough, Ontario
M1W 2T8